The Giant
Who Had No Heart

retold and illustrated by

Linda Allen

PHILOMEL BOOKS

New York

Text and illustrations copyright © 1988 by Linda Allen.
All rights reserved. Published by Philomel Books,
a division of The Putnam & Grosset Group,
51 Madison Avenue, New York, NY 10010.
Printed in Hong Kong by South China Printing Co.
Type design by Jackie Schuman.

First impression

Library of Congress Cataloging-in-Publication Data

The Giant who had no heart.

Summary: The youngest son of a king goes in
search of his missing six brothers who, together
with their brides, have been turned to stone by
a giant who has no heart.
[1. Fairy tales. 2. Folklore—Norway]
I. Allen, Linda.
PZ8.G3484 1987 398.2'1'09481 [E] 86-30371
ISBN 0-399-21446-1

To my parents, with love

There once was a king who had seven sons. He loved them so much that he could never be apart from all of them at once. Always he had to have at least one of them with him. When they were grown up, the six oldest set out to find brides. The youngest, Ashiepattle, stayed with his father, and the others were to bring back a princess for him to marry. The king gave the six the finest clothes you ever set eyes upon and the finest horses, and so they set out on their journey.

After having been to many royal palaces and seen many royal princesses, they came at last to a king who had six daughters. Such lovely princesses they had never seen before, so each of them began wooing one of the six.

When they had gotten them for sweethearts, they set out for home again, but so in love were they, they completely forgot to find a princess for Ashiepattle. When they had journeyed a good bit of the way, they passed close to the side of a steep mountain where there stood a castle that belonged to a wicked giant. As soon as the giant saw them, he came out and turned them all, princes and princesses, into stone.

At home the king waited and waited for his six sons to return, but no sons came. "Had you not been left to me," he said to Ashiepattle, "I should not care to live any longer." Now, Ashiepattle had been hoping to go and look for his brothers, and he told his father so. "I cannot let you go," said his father. "I shall lose you as well." But Ashiepattle would go, and he begged and prayed until his father finally gave him leave.

The king had no other horse left to give him but an old nag, but Ashiepattle did not mind that. "Goodbye, Father," he said to the king. "I shall come back, sure enough, and I shall bring my six brothers with me as well."

When he had gone a bit on his way, he came upon a raven lying in the road, flapping his wings, unable to get out of the way, it was so thirsty. "Dear friend, give me something to drink, and I will help you in your utmost need," said the raven.

"You don't look as if you could help me much," said Ashiepattle to the raven, "but as you're so thirsty, I'll give you what little I can." And with that, he gave the raven some of his water.

When he had traveled a bit farther, he came to a stream. On its shore there lay a salmon, dashing and knocking himself about, unable to get back into the water. "Dear friend, put me back into the water, and I will help you in your utmost need," said the salmon.

"You don't look as if you could help me much," said Ashiepattle to the salmon, "but as I can't refuse a creature in need, I'll do what little I can." And with that, he tossed the salmon into the stream.

When he had traveled some distance farther, he met a wolf who was so famished he was only able to drag himself along the road. "Dear friend, I am so hungry I can hear the wind whistling in my empty stomach. If you will give me something to eat, I will help you in your utmost need."

Now, Ashiepattle looked at the skinny wolf and said, "You don't look as if you could help me much, but as you're so hungry, I'll give you what little I can." And with that, Ashiepattle climbed down from his horse to feed the wolf. But when Ashiepattle let go of the reins, the horse galloped off into the woods as quickly as his old legs could carry him. "Now what am I to do?" moaned Ashiepattle. "I am far from home with no food and no horse."

"Climb upon my back," said the wolf, "and I will show you where your brothers are." Then the wolf set off with the prince as if he weighed nothing at all.

After a bit, they came to a castle. "There you see all your six brothers and their six brides whom the giant has turned into stone," said the wolf. "Yonder is the door of the castle. Enter there and you will meet a princess. She will tell you what to do to make the giant free your brothers and their brides." Ashiepattle went into the castle, feeling rather afraid. The giant was out, but in a chamber sat a princess, just as the wolf had said.

"Good heavens! What has brought you here?" asked the princess as soon as she saw him.

"I must see if I can free my brothers and their brides who are standing outside turned into stone."

"You'll never get the giant to do that, for he hasn't got a heart. But since you are here, we must do the best we can," said the princess. "You must creep under the bed there and listen to what the giant says when I speak with him. Be sure to lie as quiet as you can, for if he finds you, he's sure to turn you into stone as well."

Ashiepattle crept under the bed, and no sooner had he done so than the giant came home. "Ugh, what a smell of human blood there is here," shouted the giant.

"Yes, a magpie flew over the house with a man's bone and let it fall down the chimney," said the princess. Satisfied, the giant said no more about it, and when evening came, they went to their beds. When they had rested awhile, the princess said, "There is one thing I want so very much to ask you. I should like to know where your heart is since you don't carry it about with you."

"Oh, don't worry about that," said the giant, "but if you must know, it's under the stone slab in front of the door."

"Ah, ha! We shall soon see if we can't find that," said Ashiepattle to himself.

Next morning, the giant got up very early and set out for the wood. No sooner was he out of sight than Ashiepattle and the princess commenced looking for the heart under the door slab. But although they dug and searched all they could, they found nothing. "He has made a fool of me this time," said the princess, "but I will try again."

She picked the prettiest flowers she could find and strewed them over the door slab. When the time came for the giant to return home, Ashiepattle again crept under the bed. Scarcely was he well under before the giant came in.

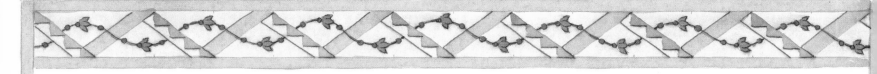

"Ugh, what a smell of human blood there is here!" bellowed the giant.

"Yes, a magpie flew over and dropped a man's bone down the chimney," said the princess. Satisfied, the giant said no more, but in a little while he asked who had been strewing flowers around the door slab. "Why, I, of course," said the princess. "I am so fond of you that I couldn't help doing it when I knew your heart was lying beneath."

"Indeed," said the giant, "but it isn't there at all." When they had gone to bed in the evening, the princess asked again where his heart was. "It's over in the cupboard," said the giant.

"Ah, ha!" thought both Ashiepattle and the princess. "We'll soon find that."

Next morning the giant was early out of bed and again set out for the wood. The moment he was gone, Ashiepattle and the princess looked in the cupboard for the heart. But although they searched all they could, they found nothing. "We must try once more," said the princess. She hung flowers and garlands around the cupboard, and when evening came, Ashiepattle crept under the bed again. Shortly, the giant came in.

"Ugh! Ugh!" he roared. "What a smell of human blood there is here."

"Yes, a magpie flew past and dropped a man's bone down the chimney," said the princess. Satisfied, the giant said no more, but as soon as he saw the cupboard decked out with flowers and garlands, he asked who had done this. "I, of course," replied the princess. "I couldn't help doing it when I knew your heart was within."

"You are a foolish creature," said the giant. "You can never go where my heart is."

"Still," said the princess, "I should just like to know where it is."

The giant could refuse to tell her no longer, and he said: "Far, far away in a lake lies an island; on that island stands a church; in that church there is a well; in that well swims a duck; in that duck there is an egg; and in that egg is my heart."

Early next morning, almost before dawn, the giant again set out for the wood. "I had better start as well," said Ashiepattle to the princess. "I only wish I knew the way." Outside the castle, who should he see but the wolf waiting for him. He told the wolf what had happened and that he was now going to look for the giant's heart. The wolf told Ashiepattle to jump on his back and he would find the way. They went over hills and mountains, over fields and valleys, while the wind whistled about them. They had traveled many, many days when at last they came to the lake. The prince did not know how he would get across it, but the wolf plunged into the water with the prince on his back and swam to the island.

They came to the church and found the key for the door hanging so high, high up on the steeple that the young prince did not know how he was going to reach it. "Call your friend the raven," said the wolf, which the prince did. The raven came at once and flew up for the key, and so the prince entered the church.

When he came to the well, the duck was there just as the giant had said. Ashiepattle called and called until at last he lured her to him and caught her. But just as he was lifting her out of the water, the duck let the egg fall into the well. Ashiepattle didn't know how he was going to get it up again. "Call your friend the salmon," said the raven, which the prince did. The salmon came at once and fetched the egg from the bottom of the well.

The salmon then told Ashiepattle to squeeze the egg, and as soon as Ashiepattle squeezed it, they heard the giant scream. "Squeeze it once more," said the wolf. When the prince did so, the giant screamed still more piteously and then asked Ashiepattle not to squeeze his heart to pieces. "First, tell him to free your brothers and their brides," said the wolf.

Ashiepattle did so, and the giant promised. "Now, tell him that unless he promises to be kind to all creatures, you will squeeze his heart to pieces between your hands." Ashiepattle did so, but when the giant heard this, he got so angry he puffed up, and before anyone could say another word, he burst. And his heart did too.

So Ashiepattle climbed back on his friend the wolf and rode to the giant's castle, and there stood his brothers and their brides, all alive and well. Ashiepattle went into the castle to ask his own princess to marry him and they all set out for home.

The king was so pleased, I can tell you, when all seven of his sons came back—each with a bride—that he gave a grand wedding feast which lasted many a day. And if they have not done feasting by this time, why, they are still at it.

Cinderella is one of the best known and most universally loved fairy tales. It is also one of the oldest. A Chinese version, *Yeh Shen,* dates from the ninth century. There are, however, variations of the tale found in Europe, Asia and around the world. At the end of the ninth century, M. R. Cox collected 345 variations. In this century, Swedish folklorist Anna Brigitta Booth counted 700.

    The Giant Who Had No Heart, with Ashiepattle as its hero, is an unmistakable variant of the Cinderella tale, although it clearly contains elements of the Jack in the Beanstalk motif as well. While the familiar ashes remain only symbolically in his name, like Cinderella and Aschenputtle in the Perrault and Grimm versions, Ashiepattle is the youngest and most lowly member of the family, who rises to a test, thereby elevating himself to a new status in his family and society.